HORRID HENRY

PRANK WARS

FRANCESCA SIMON

FRANCESCA SIMON SPENT HER CHILDHOOD ON THE BEACH IN CALIFORNIA AND STARTED WRITING STORIES AT THE AGE OF EIGHT. SHE WROTE HER FIRST HORRID HENRY BOOK IN 1994. HORRID HENRY HAS GONE ON TO CONQUER THE GLOBE; HIS ADVENTURES HAVE SOLD MILLIONS OF COPIES WORLDWIDE.

FRANCESCA HAS WON THE CHILDREN'S BOOK OF THE YEAR AWARD AND IN 2009 WAS AWARDED A GOLD BLUE PETER BADGE. SHE WAS ALSO A TRUSTEE OF THE WORLD BOOK DAY CHARITY FOR SIX YEARS.

FRANCESCA LIVES IN NORTH LONDON WITH HER FAMILY.

WWW.FRANCESCASIMON.COM WWW.HORRIDHENRY.CO.UK @SIMON_FRANCESCA

TONY ROSS

TONY ROSS WAS BORN IN LONDON AND STUDIED AT THE LIVERPOOL SCHOOL OF ART AND DESIGN. HE HAS WORKED AS A CARTOONIST, A GRAPHIC DESIGNER, AN ADVERTISING ART DIRECTOR AND A UNIVERSITY LECTURER.

TONY IS ONE OF THE MOST POPULAR AND SUCCESSFUL CHILDREN'S ILLUSTRATORS OF ALL TIME, BEST KNOWN FOR ILLUSTRATING HORRID HENRY AND THE WORKS OF DAVID WALLIAMS, AS WELL AS HIS OWN HUGELY POPULAR SERIES, THE LITTLE PRINCESS. HE LIVES IN MACCLESFIELD.

HORRID HENRY

PRANK WARS

FRANCESCA SIMON

ILLUSTRATED BY TONY ROSS

Orion

ORION CHILDREN'S BOOKS

Stories originally published in "Horrid Henry: Nits, Nits, Nits!", "Horrid Henry: Football Fiend", "Horrid Henry: Zombie Vampire", "Horrid Henry: Monster Movie", "Horrid Henry: Krazy Ketchup" and "Horrid Henry: Cannibal Curse" respectively.

This collection first published in Great Britain in 2022 by Hodder & Stoughton

1 3 5 7 9 10 8 6 4 2

Text © Francesca Simon 1997, 2006, 2011, 2012, 2014, 2015
Illustrations © Tony Ross 1997, 2006, 2011, 2012, 2014, 2015
Puzzles and activities © Orion Children's Books, 2022
Additional images © Shutterstock

The rights of Francesca Simon and Tony Ross to be identified as author and illustrator of this work have been asserted.

A CIP catalogue record for this book is available from the British Library.

ISBN 978 1 51010 968 1

Printed and bound in Great Britain by Clays Ltd, Elcograf S.p.A.

The paper and board used in this book are from well-managed forests and other responsible sources.

Orion Children's Books
An imprint of
Hachette Children's Group
Part of Hodder & Stoughton
Carmelite House
50 Victoria Embankment
London EC4Y 0DZ

An Hachette UK Company
www.hachette.co.uk

www.hachettechildrens.co.uk
www.horridhenry.co.uk

CONTENTS

HORRID HENRY

AND THE FANGMANGLER

Horrid Henry SNATCHED his skeleton bank and tried to twist open the trap door. Mum was taking him to TOY HEAVEN tomorrow. At last Henry would be able to buy the toy of his dreams: a *Dungeon Drink* kit. Ha ha ha — the tricks he'd play on his family, substituting their drinks for Dungeon stinkers.

Best of all, Moody Margaret would be green with envy. She wanted a *Dungeon Drink* kit too, but she didn't have any money. He'd have one first, and no way was Margaret ever going to play with it. Except for buying the occasional sweet and a few comics, Henry had been saving his money for weeks.

Perfect Peter peeked round the door.

"I've saved £7.53," said Peter proudly, jingling his piggy bank. "More than enough to buy my nature kit.

How much do you have?"

"**MILLIONS**," said Henry.

Perfect Peter gasped.

"You do not," said Peter. "Do you?"

Henry shook his bank. A THIN rattle came from within.

"That doesn't sound like **MILLIONS**," said Peter.

"That's 'cause five pound notes don't rattle, **stupid**," said Henry.

"Mum! Henry called me **stupid**," shrieked Peter.

"Stop being **HORRID**, Henry!" shouted Mum.

Horrid Henry gave the lid of his
bank a final **YANK** and spilled the
contents on to the floor.

A **SINGLE**, solitary five pence
coin *rolled* out.

Henry's jaw **DROPPED**. He *grabbed* the
bank and *fumbled* around inside.

It was empty.

"I'VE BEEN ROBBED!"

howled Horrid Henry. "Where's my
money? Who stole my money?"

Mum ran into the room.

"What's all this fuss?"

"PETER STOLE MY MONEY!"

SCREAMED Henry. He glared at his brother. "Just wait until I get my hands on you, you little thief, I'll—"

"No one stole your money, Henry," said Mum. "You've spent it all on *sweets* and comics."

"I have not!" shrieked Henry.

Mum pointed at the **ENORMOUS** pile of comics and *sweet* wrappers littering the floor of Henry's bedroom.

"What's all that then?" asked Mum.

Horrid Henry stopped shrieking. It was true. He *had* spent all his pocket money on comics and *sweets*. He

just hadn't noticed.

"IT'S NOT FAIR!" he screamed.

"I saved all *my* pocket money, Mum," said Perfect Peter. "After all, a penny saved is a penny earned."

Mum smiled at him. "Well done, Peter. Henry, let this be a lesson to you."

"I can't wait to buy my nature kit,"
said Perfect Peter. "You should have
saved your money like I did, instead
of wasting it, Henry."

Henry **GROWLED** and *sprang* at Peter.
He was a giant bear with huge
claws.

"**YOWWWW!**" squealed Peter.

"Henry! Stop it!" shouted Mum.
"Say sorry to Peter."

"I'm not sorry!" **SCREAMED** Henry. "**I WANT MY MONEY!**"

"Any more nonsense from you,
young man, and we won't be going

15

to **TOY HEAVEN**," said Mum.

Henry scowled.

"I don't care," he muttered. What was the point of going to **TOY HEAVEN** if he couldn't buy any toys?

Horrid Henry lay on his bedroom floor kicking *sweet* wrappers. That *Dungeon Drink* kit cost £4.99. He had

to get some money by tomorrow.

The question was, how?

He could **STEAL** Peter's money. That was tempting, as he knew the secret place in Peter's *cello* case where Peter hid his bank. Wouldn't that be fun when Peter discovered his money was gone? Henry smiled.

On second thought, perhaps not. Mum and Dad would be sure to suspect Henry, especially if he suddenly had money and Peter didn't.

He could sell some of his comics to Moody Margaret.

"**NO!**" shrieked Henry, clutching his comics to his chest. Not his **precious** comics. There *had* to be another way.

Then Henry had a wonderful, spectacular idea. It was so superb that he did a wild war dance for joy. That **Dungeon Drink** kit was as good as his. And, better still, Peter would give him all the money he needed.

Henry chortled. This would be as easy as taking sweets from a baby . . . and a lot more **FUN**.

Horrid Henry *strolled* down the hall to Peter's room. Peter was having a meeting of the Best Boys Club (motto: Can I help?) with his friends Tidy Ted, Spotless Sam and Goody-Goody Gordon. What luck. More money for him. Henry smiled as he put his ear to the keyhole and listened to them discussing their good deeds.

"I helped an old lady cross the road *and* I ate all my vegetables," said Perfect Peter.

"I kept my room tidy all week," said Tidy Ted.

"I *scrubbed* the bath without being asked," said Spotless Sam.

"I never once forgot to say *please* and *thank you*," said Goody-Goody Gordon.

Henry *PUSHED* past the barricades and **burst** into Peter's room.

"**PASSWORD!**" screeched Perfect Peter.

"Vitamins," said Horrid Henry.

"How did you know?" said Tidy Ted, staring open-mouthed at Henry.

"Never you mind," said Henry,

who was not a master spy for nothing.

"I don't suppose any of you know about Fangmanglers?"

The boys looked at one another.

"What are they?" asked Spotless Sam.

"Only the slimiest, SCARIEST, most horrible and FRIGHTENING monsters in the whole world," said Henry. "And I know where to find one."

"Where?" said Goody-Goody Gordon.

"I'm not going to tell you," said Horrid Henry.

"Oh please!" said Spotless Sam.

Henry shook his head and lowered his voice.

"Fangmanglers only come out at night," WHISPERED Henry. "They slip into the shadows then sneak out and . . . BITE YOU!" he suddenly shrieked.

The Best Boys Club members gasped with fright.

"I'm not scared," said Peter. "And I've never heard of a Fangmangler."

"That's because you're too young," said Henry. "Grown-ups don't tell you about them because they don't want to scare you."

"I want to see it," said Tidy Ted.

"Me too," said Spotless Sam and Goody-Goody Gordon.

Peter hesitated for a moment.

"Is this a trick, Henry?"

"Of course not," said Henry. "And

just for that I won't let you come."

"Oh please, Henry," said Peter.

Henry paused.

"All right," he said. "We'll meet in the back garden after dark. But it will cost you **TWO POUNDS** each."

"Two pounds!" they SQUEALED.

"Do you want to see a **Fangmangler** or don't you?"

Perfect Peter exchanged a look with his friends.

They all nodded.

"Good," said Horrid Henry. "See you at six o'clock. And don't forget to bring your money."

TEE HEE, chortled Henry silently. Eight pounds! He could get a **Dungeon Drink** kit *and* a Grisly Ghoul Grub box at this rate.

Loud screams came from next door's garden.

"GIVE ME BACK MY SPADE!" came Moody Margaret's bossy tones.

"You're so mean, Margaret," SQUEALED Sour Susan's sulky voice. "Well,

I won't. It's my turn to dig with it now."

WHACK! THWACK! "WAAAAAAA!"

Eight pounds is nice, thought **Horrid Henry**, but twelve is even nicer.

"What's going on?" asked Horrid Henry, **SMIRKING** as he leapt over the wall.

"Go away, Henry!" shouted Moody Margaret.

"Yeah, Henry," echoed Sour Susan, wiping away her **tears**. "We don't want you."

"All right," said Henry. "Then

I won't tell you about the
Fangmangler I've found."

"We don't want to know about it," said
Margaret, turning her back on him.

"That's right," said Susan.

"Well then, don't blame me when

the **Fangmangler** sneaks over the
wall and **RIPS** you to pieces and
chews up your guts," said Horrid
Henry. He turned to go.

The girls looked at one another.

"Wait," ordered Margaret.

"Yeah?" said Henry.

"You don't scare me," said
Margaret.

"Prove it then," said Henry.

"How?" said Margaret.

"Be in my
garden at
six o'clock

tonight and I'll show you the **Fangmangler**. But it will cost you two pounds each."

"Forget it," said Margaret. "Come on, Susan."

"Okay," said Henry quickly. "One pound each."

"No," said Margaret.

"And your money back if the **Fangmangler** doesn't scare you," said Henry.

Moody Margaret *smiled*.

"It's a deal," she said.

When the coast was clear, Horrid Henry crept into the bushes and hid a bag containing his supplies: an old, torn T-shirt, some **FILTHY** trousers and a jumbo-sized bottle of **ketchup**. Then he sneaked back into the house and waited for dark.

"**Thank you, thank you, thank you, thank you,**" said Horrid Henry, collecting two pounds from each member of the Best Boys Club.

Henry placed the money carefully in his skeleton bank. Boy, was he **RICH!**

Moody Margaret and Sour Susan handed over one pound each.

"Remember, Henry, we get our money back if we aren't scared," hissed Moody Margaret.

"Shut up, Margaret," said Henry. "I'm risking my life and all you can think about is money. Now everyone, wait here, don't move and don't talk," he WHISPERED. "We have to surprise the Fangmangler. If not . . ." Henry paused and drew his fingers across his

throat. "I'm a goner. I'm going off now to hunt for the **MONSTER**. When I find him, and if it's safe, I'll whistle twice. Then everyone come, as quietly as you can. But be careful!"

Henry disappeared into the black darkness of the garden.

For a **long long** moment there was silence.

"This is stupid," said Moody Margaret.

Suddenly, a **LOW**, *moaning* GROWL echoed through the moonless night.

"What was that?" said Spotless Sam nervously.

"Henry? Are you all right, Henry?" squeaked Perfect Peter.

The **LOW**, *moaning* GROWL turned into a *snarl*.

THRASH! CRASH!

"HELP! HELP! THE FANGMANGLER'S AFTER ME! RUN FOR YOUR LIVES!" screamed

Horrid Henry, *smashing* through
the bushes. His T-shirt and
trousers were torn. There was **blood**
everywhere.

The Best Boys Club **SCREAMED** and
ran.

Sour Susan **SCREAMED** and ran.

Moody Margaret **SCREAMED** and
ran.

Horrid Henry **SCREAMED** and . . .
stopped.

He waited until he was alone. Then
Horrid Henry wiped some **ketchup**
from his face, clutched his piggy

bank and did a **WAR** dance round the garden, whooping with joy.

"**MONEY! MONEY! MONEY! MONEY! MONEY!**" he SQUEALED, leaping and stomping. He danced and he pranced, he twirled and he whirled. He was so busy dancing and cackling he didn't notice a shadowy shape slip into the garden behind him.

"**MONEY! MONEY! MONEY! MINE! MINE—**"

He broke off. What was that noise?
Horrid Henry's throat tightened.

Nah, he thought. It's nothing.

Then suddenly a dark shape leapt
out of the bushes and let out a
THUNDEROUS roar.

Horrid Henry **SHRIEKED** with terror.
He dropped his money and ran for
his life. **The Thing** scooped up his
bank and slithered over the wall.

Horrid Henry did not stop running
until he was safely in his room with
the door shut tight and barricaded.

His heart **POUNDED**.

There really is a **Fangmangler**, he
thought, TREMBLING. And now it's
after **me**.

Horrid Henry hardly slept a wink.
He started awake at every *squeak*
and *creak*. He shook and he **SHRIEKED**.
Henry had such a bad night that he
slept in quite late the next morning,
tossing and turning.

FIZZ! POP! GURGLE! BANG!

Henry jerked awake. What was
that? He peeked his head out from
under the duvet and listened.

FIZZ! POP! GURGLE! BANG!

Those FIZZING and POPPING noises seemed to be coming from next door.

Henry ran to the window and pulled open the curtains. There was Moody Margaret sitting beside a large TOY HEAVEN bag. In front of her was . . . a Dungeon Drink kit. She saw him, smiled and raised a glass of BUBBLING black liquid.

"Want a Fangmangler drink, Henry?" asked Margaret sweetly.

HORRID HENRY

PEEKS AT PETER'S DIARY

"**What are you doing?**" demanded **Horrid Henry**, bursting into **Peter's bedroom**.

"Nothing," said Perfect Peter quickly, slamming his notebook shut.

"Yes you are," said Henry.

"Get out of my room," said Peter. "You're not allowed to come in unless I say so."

Horrid Henry leaned over Peter's shoulder.

"What are you **WRITING**?"

"None of your business," said Peter.

He covered the closed notebook tightly with his arm.

"It is **too** my business if you're writing about me."

"It's my diary. I can write what I want to," said Peter. "Miss Lovely said we should keep a diary for a week and write in it every day."

"**BO-RING**," said Henry, yawning.

"No it isn't," said Peter. "Anyway, you'll find out next week what I'm **WRITING**: I've been chosen to read my diary **out loud** for our class assembly."

Horrid Henry's heart turned to ice.

Peter read his diary **out loud**? So the whole school could hear Peter's lies about him? No way!

"GIMME THAT!" screamed Horid Henry, *lunging* for the diary.

"No!" screamed Peter, holding on tight. "MUUUM! Help! Henry's in my room! And he didn't knock! And he won't leave!"

"Shut up, TATTLE-TALE," hissed Henry, forcing Peter's fingers off the diary.

"MUUUUMMMMMM!" shrieked Peter. Mum **stomped** up the stairs.

Henry opened the diary. But before he could read a single word Mum BURST in.

"He snatched my diary! And he told me to shut up!" wailed Peter.

"Henry! Stop annoying your brother," said Mum.

"I wasn't," said Henry.

"Yes he was," snivelled Peter.

"And now you've made him cry," said Mum. "Say sorry."

"I was just asking about his

homework," protested Henry *innocently*.

"He was trying to read my diary," said Peter.

"**HENRY!**" said Mum. "Don't be **horrid**. A diary is private. Now leave your brother alone."

It was so unfair. Why did Mum always believe Peter?

HUMPH. Horrid Henry stalked out of Peter's bedroom. Well, no way was Henry waiting until class assembly to find out what Peter had written.

SNEAK. SNEAK. SNEAK.

Horrid Henry checked to the
right. Horrid Henry checked to the
left. Mum was downstairs working on
the computer. Dad was in the garden.
Peter was playing at Goody-Goody
Gordon's house.

At last, the coast was clear. He'd
been trying to get hold of Peter's
diary for days. There was no time
to lose.

Tomorrow was Peter's class
assembly. Would he mention Sunday's
food fight, when Henry had been

forced to throw soggy pasta at Peter?
Or when Henry had to *push* Peter off
the comfy black chair and pinch him?
Or yesterday when Henry banished
him from the PURPLE HAND CLUB and
Peter had run SCREAMING
to Mum?

A lying, **slimy worm** like Peter would be sure to make it look like Henry was the VILLAIN when in fact Peter was always to blame.

Even worse, what **horrid** lies had Peter been making up about him? People would read Peter's ravings and think they were true. When Henry was *famous*, books would be written about him, and someone would find Peter's diary and believe it! When things were written down they had a **horrible** way of seeming to be true even when they were **BIG FAT LIES**.

Henry SNEAKED into Peter's bedroom and shut the door. Now, where was that diary? Henry glanced at Peter's tidy desk. Peter kept it on the second shelf, next to his crayons and trophies.

The diary was gone.

RATS. Peter must have hidden it.

That little worm, thought Horrid Henry. Why on earth would he hide his diary? And where on earth would that smelly toad hide it? Behind his "Good as Gold" certificates? In the laundry basket? Underneath his stamp collection?

He checked Peter's sock drawer.
No diary.

He checked Peter's underwear
drawer. No diary.

He PEEKED UNDER Peter's pillow and
UNDER Peter's bed.

Still no diary.

Okay, where would I hide a diary?
thought Horrid Henry desperately.
Easy. I'd put it in a chest and bury

it in the garden, with a **PIRATE CURSE** on it.

Somehow he doubted Perfect Peter would be so clever.

Okay, thought Henry, if I were an *ugly toad* like him, where would I hide it?

The bookcase. Of course. What better place to hide a book?

Henry *strolled* over to Peter's bookcase, with all the books arranged neatly in alphabetical order. **AHA!** What was that sticking out between

The Happy Nappy and THE HOPPY HIPPO?

Gotcha, thought Horrid Henry, yanking the diary off the shelf. At last he would know Peter's secrets. He'd make him cross out all his lies if it was the last thing he did.

Horrid Henry sat down and began to read:

Monday

Today I drew a picture of my teacher, Miss Lovely. Miss Lovely gave me a gold star for reading. That's because I'm the best reader in the class. And the best at maths. And the best at everything else.

Tuesday

Today I said please and thank you 236 times

Wednesday

Today I ate all my vegetables

Thursday
Today I sharpened my pencils.
I ate all my sprouts and had
seconds.

Friday
Today I wrote a poem to my mummy

    I Love my mummy,
    I came out of her tummy,
    Her food is yummy,
    She is so scrummy,
    I love my mummy.

Slowly Horrid Henry closed Peter's diary. He knew Peter's diary would be bad. But never in his **WORST** nightmares had he imagined anything this **BAD**.

Perfect Peter hadn't mentioned him once. Not once.

You'd think I didn't even live in this house, thought Henry. He was **OUTRAGED**. How dare Peter not write about him? And then all the **stupid** things Peter had written.

Henry's name would be **mud** when people heard Peter's diary in assembly and found out what a sad brother he had. Everyone would tease him. Horrid Henry would never live down the shame.

Peter needed Henry's help, and he

needed it fast. Horrid
Henry grabbed a
pencil and got to work.

<u>Monday</u>
Today I drew a picture of my teacher,
Miss Lovely. I drew her with Piggy
ears and a grate big giant belly
Then I turned it into a
dartbord Miss Lovely gave me
a gold star for reading. Miss
Lovely is my worst teecher
ever. She should reely be
called Miss Lumpy.

Miss Dumpy Lumpy is wot Gordon and I call her behind her back. Tee hee, she'll never know!

I'm the best reader in the class. And the best at maths. And the best at everything else. Too bad I have smelly pants and nitty hair

Tuesday
Today I said please and thank you 236 times

~~Fals~~ Not! I called Mum a big blobby pants face. I called Dad a stinky fish. Then I played Pirats with the worlds greatest brother, Henry. I wish I were as clever as Henry. But I know thats imposibel.

Wednesday

Today I ate all my vegetables

then I sneeked loads of sweets from the sweet Jar and lied to dad about it. I am a very good liar. No one should ever beleeve a word I say. Henry gets the blame but reely everything is always my fault.

Thursday

Today I sharpened my pencils.

All the better to write rude notes!

I ate all my sprouts and had seconds. then threw up all over Mum. Eeugh, what a smell. I reely am a smelly toad. I am so lucky to have a grate brother like Henry. He is always so nice to me Hip Hip Hurray for Henry

Friday
Today I wrote a poem to my Dummy

I Love my Dummy,
It's my best chummy
It tastes so yummy,
It is so scrummy,
I love my Dummy.

Much better, thought Horrid Henry. Now that's what I call a diary. Everyone would have **DIED** of boredom otherwise.

Henry carefully replaced Peter's diary in the bookcase. I hope Peter appreciates what I've done for him, thought Horrid Henry.

The entire school gathered in the hall for assembly. Peter's class sat *proudly* on benches at the front. Henry's class sat cross-legged on the floor. The parents sat on chairs down both sides.

Mum and Dad *waved* at Peter. He *waved* shyly back.

Miss Lovely stood up.

"Hello, mums and dads, boys and girls, welcome to our class assembly. This term our class has been keeping diaries. We're going to read some of them to you now. First to read will be *Peter.* Everyone pay attention, and see

if you too can be as good as I know
Peter has been. I'd like everyone here
to copy one of Peter's good deeds. I
know I can't wait to hear how he has
spent this last week."

Peter stood up, and opened his
diary. In a **BIG LOUD** voice, he read:

"MONDAY. Today I drew a picture of
my teacher, Miss Lovely."

Peter glanced up at Miss Lovely.
She *beamed* at him.

"I drew her with piggy ears and a
great big giant belly. Then I turned it
into a dartboard."

What??! It was always difficult to read out loud and understand what he had read, but something didn't sound right. He didn't remember writing about a **pig** with a **big belly**.

Nervously Peter looked up at Mum and Dad. Was he imagining it, or did their smiles seem more like FROWNS? Peter shook his head, and carried on.

"Miss Lovely gave me a GOLD STAR for reading."

Phew, that was better! He must have misheard himself before.

"Miss Lovely is my WORST teacher ever. She should really be called Miss Lumpy. Miss Dumpy Lumpy—"

"Thank you, that's quite enough," interrupted Miss Lovely sternly, as the school erupted in SHRIEKS of

laughter. Her face was pink. "Peter, see me after assembly. Ted will now tell us all about **skeletons.**"

"But — but—" gasped Perfect Peter. "I — I didn't, I never—"

"SIT DOWN AND BE QUIET," said the head, Mrs Oddbod. "I'll see you and your parents later."

"WAAAAAAAAAA!" wailed Peter.

Mum and Dad stared at their feet. Why had they ever had children?

Where was a **TRAPDOOR** when you
needed one?

"WAAAAAAAA," whimpered Mum
and Dad.

Naturally, Henry got into trouble. **Big big trouble**. It was so unfair. Why didn't anyone believe him when he said he'd improved Peter's diary for his own good? **Honestly, he would never ever do Peter a favour again.**

HORRID HENRY

AND THE ZOMBIE VAMPIRE

"Isn't it exciting, Henry?" said Perfect Peter, packing Bunnykins carefully in his Sammy the Snail overnight bag.

"A museum sleepover! With a torch-lit trail! And worksheets! I can't think of anything more fun."

"I can," snarled **Horrid Henry**.

Being trapped in a cave with Clever Clare reciting all the multiplication tables from one to a million. Watching **Cooking Cuties**. Even visiting NurseNeedleforoneofher **HORRIBLE**

injections. (Well, maybe not that.)

But almost anything would be better than being stuck overnight in *Our Town Museum* on a class sleepover. **NO TV**. No COMPUTERS. **NO COMICS**. Why oh why did he have to do this? He wanted to sleep in his own comfy bed, not in a sleeping bag on the museum's cold, hard floor, surrounded by photos of old mayors and a few dusty exhibits.

AAARRRGGGHH. Wasn't it bad enough he was **bored** all day in school without being **bored** all night too?

Worse, Peter's nappy baby class was coming, too. They'd probably have to be tucked in at seven o'clock, when they'd all start crying for their mamas. UGGHH. And then MISS BATTLE-AXE snarling at them to finish their worksheets, and MOODY MARGARET snoring, and Anxious Andrew whimpering that he'd seen a ghost . . .

Well, no way was Henry going to that BORING OLD DUMP without some comics to pass the time.

Waaaaaaaa!

He'd just bought the latest **Screamin'
Demon**, with a big article all about
vampires and zombies. Yay! He
couldn't wait to read it.

Perfect Peter watched him stuff his
Mutant Max bag full of comics.

"Henry, you know we're not allowed
to bring comics to the museum
sleepover," said Perfect Peter.

"Shut up and mind your own
business, **toad**," said Horrid Henry.

"Mum! Henry just called me a
toad!" wailed Peter. "And he told
me to shut up."

"*Toady Toady Toady, Toady Toady Toady*," jeered Henry.

"Henry! Stop being **HORRID** or no museum sleepover for you," yelled Mum.

Horrid Henry paused. Was it too late to be horrid enough to get banned from the sleepover? Why hadn't he thought of this before? Why, he could . . .

"Henry! Peter! We have to leave now!" yelled Dad.

RATS.

73

The children queued up in the
museum's *Central Hall* clutching
their sleeping bags as Miss Lovely
and **MISS BATTLE-AXE** ticked off names
on a big register.

"Go away, Susan," said **MOODY**
MARGARET. "After what you did at my

house I'm going to sit with Gurinder.
So there."

"You're such a **meanie**, Margaret,"
said Sour Susan.

"Am not."

"Are too."

Susan scowled. Margaret was always
so mean. If only she could think of a
way to pay that old grouch back.

Margaret **scowled**. Susan was
always so annoying. If only she could
think of a way to pay that old fraidy
cat back.

Henry **scowled**. Why did he have

to be here? What he'd give for a **MAGIC CARPET** to whisk him straight home to the comfy **BLACK** chair to watch **Terminator Gladiator**. Could life get any worse?

"Henwy," came a little voice next to him. "I love you, Henwy. I want to give you a big kiss."

Oh no, thought **Horrid Henry**. Oh no. It was Lisping Lily, New Nick's

little sister. What was that foul fiend
doing here?

"You keep away from me," said
Horrid Henry, *pushing* and **shoving**
his way through the children to
escape her.

"Waaa!" wept Weepy William as
Henry stepped on his foot.

"I want my mama," cried Needy
Neil as Henry trampled on his
sleeping bag.

"But I want to marry with you,
Henwy," lisped Lily, trying to follow
him.

"HENRY! STAY STILL!" barked Miss Battle-Axe, glaring at him with her demon eyes.

"Hello, boys and girls. What an adventure we're going to have tonight," said the museum's guide, Earnest Ella, as she handed out pencils and worksheets. Henry groaned. **BORING!** He hated worksheets.

"Did you know that our museum has a famous collection of balls of wool through the ages?" droned Earnest Ella. "And an old railway

car? Oh yes, it's going to be an exciting sleepover. We're even going on a torch-lit walk through the corridors."

Horrid Henry yawned and sneaked a peek at his **COMIC** book, which he'd hidden beneath his museum worksheet.

Watch out, Demon fans!! To celebrate the release of this season's big blockbuster monster horror film, THE ZOMBIE VAMPIRES, study this checklist. Make sure there are

no zombie vampires lurking in your neighbourhood!!!!

Horrid Henry gasped as he read HOW TO RECOGNISE A VAMPIRE and HOW TO RECOGNISE A ZOMBIE. Big scary teeth? Big googly eyes? Looks like the walking dead? Wow, that described **MISS BATTLE-AXE** perfectly. All they had to add was "big fat carrot nose" and . . .

A dark shadow loomed over him.

"I'll take that," snapped Miss Battle-Axe, yanking the comic out of his hand. "And the rest."

Huh?

He'd been so careful. How had she spotted that comic under his worksheet? And how did she know about the secret stash in his bag? **Horrid Henry** looked round the hall. Aha! There was Peter, pretending not to look at him. How dare that *wormy worm toad* tell on him? Just for that . . .

"Come along, everyone, line up to collect your torches for our *spooky* walk," said Earnest Ella. "You wouldn't want to get left behind in the dark, would you?"

There was no time to lose. Horrid Henry *slipped* over to Peter's class and joined him in line with Tidy Ted and Goody-Goody Gordon.

"Hello, Peter," said Henry sweetly.

Peter looked at him nervously. Did Henry suspect he'd told on him? Henry didn't look angry.

"Shame my COMIC got

confiscated," said Henry, "'cause it had a list of how to tell whether anyone you know is a **zombie vampire**."

"A zombie vampire?" said Tidy Ted.

"Yup," said Henry.

"They're imaginary," said Goody-Goody Gordon.

"That's what they'd like you to believe," said Henry. "But I've discovered some."

"Where?" said Ted.

Horrid Henry looked around dramatically, then dropped his voice to a whisper.

"Two teachers at our school,"
hissed Henry.

"Two teachers?" said Peter.

"What?" said Ted.

"You heard me. **Zombie vampires**.
MISS BATTLE-AXE and **Miss Lovely**."

"Miss Lovely?" gasped Peter.

"You're just making that up," said
Gordon.

"It was all in **Screamin' Demon**,"

said Henry. "That's why Miss Battle-
Axe snatched my comic. To stop me
finding out the truth. Listen carefully."

Henry recited:

"How to recognise a vampire:

"1. BIG HUGE SCARY TEETH.

"If Miss Battle-Axe's fangs were any
bigger she would trip over them," said
Horrid Henry.

Tidy Ted nodded. "She does have big
pointy teeth."

"That doesn't prove anything," said
Peter.

"2. DRINKS BLOOD."

Perfect Peter shook his head. "Drinks . . . blood?"

"Obviously they do, just not in front of people," said Horrid Henry. "That would give away their terrible secret.

3. ONLY APPEARS AT NIGHT."

"But Henry," said Goody-Goody Gordon, "we see Miss Battle-Axe and Miss Lovely every day at school. They can't be vampires."

Henry sighed. "Have you been paying attention? I didn't say they were vampires, I said they were **zombie vampires.** Being half zombie

lets them walk about in daylight."

Perfect Peter and Goody-Goody Gordon looked at one another.

"Here's the total proof," Henry continued.

"How to recognise a zombie:

"1. LOOKS DEAD.

"Does Miss Battle-Axe look dead? Definitely," said Horrid Henry. "I never saw a more dead-looking person."

"But Henry," said Peter, "she's alive."

Unfortunately, yes, thought Horrid Henry.

"Duh," he said. "Zombies always seem alive. Plus, zombies have got scary bulging eyes like **MISS BATTLE-AXE**," continued Henry. "And they feed on human flesh."

"Miss Lovely doesn't eat human flesh," said Peter. "She's a *vegetarian*."

"A likely story," said Henry.

"You're just trying to scare us," said Peter.

"Don't you see?" said Henry. "They're planning to *pounce* on us during the torch-lit trail."

"I don't believe you," said Peter.

Henry shrugged. "Fine. Don't believe me. Just don't say I didn't warn you when *Miss Lovely* lurches out of the dark and **BITES** you!" he shrieked.

"**BE QUIET, HENRY**," shouted Miss Battle-Axe. "William. Stop weeping. There's nothing to be scared of. Linda! Stand up. It's not bedtime yet. Bert! Where's your torch?"

"I dunno," said Beefy Bert.

Miss Lovely walked over and smiled at Peter.

"Looking forward to the torch-lit walk?" she beamed.

Peter couldn't stop himself sneaking a peek at her teeth. Were they **big?** And **sharp?** Funny, he'd never noticed before how pointy two of them were . . . And was her face a bit . . . umm . . . PALE?

No! Henry was just trying to trick him. Well, he wasn't going to be fooled.

"Time to go exploring," said Earnest Ella. "First stop on the torch-lit trail:

our brand-new exhibit, *Wonderful World of Wool*. Then we'll be popping next door down the Passage to the Past to visit the old railway car and the Victorian shop and a Neanderthal cave. Torches on, everyone."

Sour Susan smiled to herself. She'd just thought of the perfect revenge on Margaret for being so mean to her.

Moody Margaret smiled to herself. She'd just thought of the perfect revenge on Susan for being so sour.

HA HA, Margaret, thought Susan. I'll get you tonight.

HA HA, Susan, thought Margaret. I'll get you tonight.

Ha ha, Peter, thought Henry. I'll get you tonight.

"Follow me," said Earnest Ella.

The children stampeded after her. All except three.

When the coast was clear, **MOODY MARGARET** turned off her torch, darted into the pitch-black Passage to the Past hall and hid in the Neanderthal cave behind the caveman. She'd leap out at Susan when she walked past. **MWAHAHAHAHAHAHA!** Wouldn't that old scaredy cat get a fright?

Sour Susan turned off her torch and peeked down the Passage to the Past corridor. Empty. She TIPTOED to the railway car and crept inside. Just

wait till Margaret walked by . . .

Horrid Henry turned off his torch, crept down the Passage to the Past, sneaked into the Victorian shop and hid behind the rocking chair.

Tee hee. Just wait till Peter

walked past. He'd—

What was that?

Was it his imagination? Or did that spinning wheel in the corner of the shop . . . move?

CR—EEEAK went the wheel.

It was so dark. But Henry didn't dare switch on his torch.

MOODY MARGARET looked over from the Neanderthal cave at the Victorian shop. Was it her imagination or was that

rocking chair rocking *back* and *forth?*

Sour Susan looked out from the railway car. Was it her imagination or was the caveman moving?

There was a strange, scuttling noise.

What was that? thought Susan.

You know, thought Henry, this museum is kind of creepy at night.

And then something grabbed on to his leg.

"AAAARRRGGHH!"

screamed Horrid Henry.

MOODY MARGARET heard a **blood-curdling SCREAM**. Scarcely daring to breathe, Margaret peeped over the caveman's shoulder . . .

Sour Susan heard a **blood-curdling SCREAM**. Scarcely daring to breathe, Susan peeped out from the railway carriage . . .

"Henwy, I found you, Henwy," piped the creature clinging to his leg.

"Go away, Lily," hissed Henry. The **horrible fiend** was going to ruin everything.

"Will you marry me, Henwy?"

"**NO**!" said Horrid Henry, trying to shake her off and brushing against the spinning wheel.

CR-EEEAK.

The spinning wheel spun.

What's that noise? thought Margaret, craning to see from behind the caveman.

"Henwy! I want to give you a big kiss," lisped Lily.

Horrid Henry shook his leg harder.

The spinning wheel tottered and fell

over.

CRASH!

Margaret and Susan saw something

lurch out of the Victorian shop and loom

up in the darkness. A **MONSTROUS**

creature with four legs and waving

arms . . .

"AAAARRRRGGHH!" screamed Susan.

"AAAARGGHHHHH!" shrieked Margaret.

"AAAARGGHHHHH!" shrieked Henry.

The unearthly screams rang through the museum. Peter, Ted and Gordon froze.

"You don't think—" gasped Gordon.

"Not . . ." trembled Peter.

"Zombie vampires?" whimpered Ted. They clutched one another.

"Everyone head back to the Central Hall NOW!" shouted Earnest Ella.

In the cafeteria, Miss Lovely and **MISS BATTLE-AXE** were snatching a short break to enjoy a *lovely* fried egg sandwich with lashings of **ketchup**.

Oh my weary bones, thought Miss Battle-Axe, as she sank her teeth into the huge sandwich. Peace at last.

"AAARRGGHH!

EEEEEKKK! HELLLP!"

MISS BATTLE-AXE and Miss Lovely squeezed their sandwiches in shock as they heard the terrible screams.

SPLAT!

A stream of ketchup squirted Miss Lovely in the eye and dripped down her face on to her blouse.

SQUIRT!

A blob of **ketchup** splatted Miss Battle-Axe on the nose and dribbled down her chin on to her cardigan.

"Sorry, Boudicca," said Miss Lovely.

"Sorry, Lydia," said Miss Battle-Axe.

They *raced* into the dark Central
Hall just as their classes ran back
from the torch-lit walk. Fifty beams
of light from fifty torches lit up the
teachers' ketchup-covered faces and
ketchup-stained clothes.

"AAAARRGGHHH!"
screamed Perfect Peter.

"It's the **zombie vampires!**" howled Tidy Ted.

"RUN FOR YOUR LIVES!"
yelped Goody-Goody Gordon.

"Wait!" shouted Miss Lovely. "Children, come back!"

"We won't eat you!" shouted Miss Battle-Axe.

"AAAARRRRGGHHHHHH!"

HORRID HENRY'S

HORRID WEEKEND

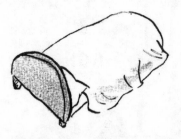

"**NOOOOOOOOO!**" screamed
Horrid Henry. "I don't
want to spend the
weekend with Steve."

"Don't be **HORRID**, Henry," said
Mum. "It's very kind of Aunt Ruby to
invite us down for the weekend."

"But I **HATE** Aunt Ruby!"
shrieked Henry. "And I hate Steve
and I hate you!"

"I can't wait to go," said Perfect Peter.

"**Shut up, Peter!**" howled Henry.

"Don't tell your brother to shut up,"
shouted Mum.

"**SHUT UP! SHUT UP! SHUT UP!**" And **Horrid Henry** fell to the floor wailing and screaming and kicking.

STUCK-UP STEVE was Horrid Henry's hideous cousin. Steve hated Henry. Henry hated him. The last time Henry had seen Steve, Henry had **tricked** him into thinking there was a monster under his bed. Steve had sworn revenge. Then there was the other time at the restaurant when . . . well, **Horrid Henry** thought it would

be a good
idea to avoid
Steve until his

cousin was grown-up and in prison for
CRIMES AGAINST HUMANITY.

And now his MEAN, HORRIBLE
parents were forcing him to spend
a whole precious weekend with the
toadiest, *wormiest*, smelliest boy who
ever slimed out of a swamp.

Mum sighed. "We're going and that's
that. Ruby says Steve is having a lovely
friend over so that should be extra fun."

Henry stopped screaming and

kicking. Maybe Steve's friend wouldn't be a stuck-up **MONSTER**. Maybe he'd been forced to waste his weekend with Steve, too. After all, who'd volunteer to spend time with Steve? Maybe together they could squish **STUCK-UP STEVE** once and for all.

DING DONG.

Horrid Henry, Perfect Peter, Mum and Dad stood outside Rich Aunt Ruby's **ENORMOUS** house on a

grey, drizzly day. Steve opened the **massive** front door.

"Oh," he sneered. "It's you."

Steve opened the present Mum had brought. It was a SMALL flashlight. Steve put it down.

"I already have a much better one," he said.

"Oh," said Mum.

Another boy stood beside him. A boy who looked vaguely familiar. A boy . . . **Horrid Henry** gasped. Oh no. It was Bill. **Bossy Bill**. The **HORRIBLE** son of Dad's boss.

Henry had once **tricked** Bill into photocopying his bottom. Bill had sworn revenge. **Horrid Henry's** insides turned to jelly. Trust **STUCK-UP STEVE** to be friends with **Bossy Bill**. It was bad enough being trapped in a house with one arch-enemy. Now he was stuck in a house with TWO . . .

Stuck-up Steve **SCOWLED** at Henry. "You're wearing that old shirt of mine," he said. "Don't your parents ever buy you new clothes?"

Bossy Bill snorted.

"Steve," said Aunt Ruby. "Don't be rude."

"I wasn't," said Steve. "I was just asking. No harm in asking, is there?"

"No," said Horrid Henry. He smiled at Steve. "So when will Aunt Ruby buy you a new face?"

"**HENRY**," said Mum. "Don't be rude."

"I was just asking," said Henry. "No harm in asking, is there?" he added, glaring at Steve.

Steve *glared* back.

Aunt Ruby beamed. "Henry, Steve and Bill are taking you to their friend Tim's 𝕻𝔸𝕀𝕹𝕋𝔹𝔸𝕃𝕃𝕀𝕹𝔾 party."

"Won't that be FUN," said Mum.

Peter looked frightened.

"Don't worry, Peter," said Aunt Ruby, "you can help me plant seedlings while the older boys are out."

Peter beamed. "Thank you," he said. "I don't like PAINTBALLING. Too messy and scary."

Paintballing! **Horrid Henry** loved paintballing. The chance to **splat** Steve and Bill with OOEY GOOEY GLOBS of paint . . . hmmm, maybe the weekend was looking up.

"Great!" said Horrid Henry.

"How nice," said Rich Aunt Ruby, "you boys already know each other. Think how much fun you're all going to have sharing Steve's bedroom together."

Uh-oh, thought **Horrid Henry**.

"Yeah!" said Stuck-Up Steve. "We're looking forward to sharing a room with Henry." His PIGGY eyes gleamed.

"Yeah!" said Bossy Bill. "I can't wait." His piggy eyes gleamed.

"Yeah," said Horrid Henry. He wouldn't be sleeping a wink.

Horrid Henry looked around the **enormous** high-ceilinged bedroom he'd be sharing with his two evil enemies for two very long days and one very long night. There was a bunk-bed, which Steve and Bill had already nabbed, and two single beds. Steve's bedroom shelves were stuffed with **ZILLIONS** of new toys and games, as usual.

Bill and Steve smirked at each other. Henry **SCOWLED** at them. What were they plotting?

"Don't you dare touch my **SUPER-BLOOPER BLASTER**," said Steve.

"Don't you dare touch my **Demon Dagger Sabre**," said Bill.

A Super-Blooper Blaster! A Demon Dagger Sabre! Trust Bill and Steve to have the two best toys in the world . . . **RATS**.

"Don't worry," said Henry. "I don't play with baby toys."

"Oh yeah," said STUCK-UP STEVE. "Bet you're too much of a baby to jump off my top bunk on to your bed."

"Am not," said Henry.

"We're not allowed to jump on beds," said Perfect Peter.

"We're not allowed," mimicked Steve. "I thought you were too poor to even have beds."

"Ha ha," said Henry.

"Chicken. Chicken. Scaredy cat," sneered Bossy Bill.

"Squawk!" said Stuck-Up Steve. "I knew you'd be too scared, chicken."

That did it. No one called **Horrid Henry** chicken and lived. As if he, Henry, **LEADER OF A PIRATE GANG**, would be afraid to jump off a top bunk. Ha.

"Don't do it, Henry," said Perfect Peter.

"Shut up, **worm**," said Henry.

"But it's so high," squealed Peter, squeezing his eyes shut.

Horrid Henry clambered up the ladder and stepped on to the top

bunk.

"It's nothing," he lied. "I've jumped off **MUCH** higher."

"Well, go on then," said Stuck-Up Steve.

Boing! Horrid Henry bounced.

Boing! Horrid Henry bounced higher. **WHEE!** This bed was very springy.

"We're waiting, chicken," said Bossy
Bill.

BOING! BOING! Horrid Henry bent
his knees, then . . . leap! He jumped
on to the single bed below.

SMASH!

Horrid Henry crashed to the floor
as the bed collapsed beneath him.

Huh? What? How could he have
broken the bed? He hadn't heard any
breaking sounds.

It was as if . . . as if . . .

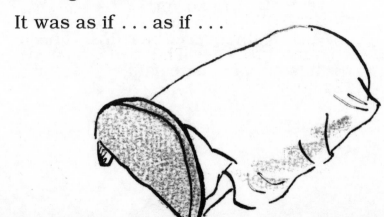

Mum, Dad and Aunt Ruby ran into the room.

"Henry broke the bed," said Stuck-Up Steve.

"We tried to stop him," said Bossy Bill, "but Henry insisted on jumping."

"But . . . but . . ." said Horrid Henry.

"Henry!" wailed Mum. "You **HORRID** boy."

"How could you be so horrid?" said Dad. "No **POCKET MONEY** for a year. Ruby, I'm so sorry."

Aunt Ruby pursed her lips. "These things happen," she said.

"And no PAINTBALLING party for you," said Mum.

What?

"No!" wailed Henry.

Then **Horrid Henry** saw a HORRIBLE sight. Behind Aunt Ruby's back, Steve and Bill were covering their mouths and laughing. Henry realised the TERRIBLE truth. Bill and Steve had tricked him. They'd broken the bed. And now he'd got the blame.

"BUT I DIDN'T BREAK IT!"

screamed Henry.

"Yes you did, Henry," said Peter.
"I saw you."

AAAARRRRGGGGHHHH!

Horrid Henry leapt at Peter. He was
a storm god hurling thunderbolts at a
foolish mortal.

"AAAIIIEEEEEE!" squealed Perfect
Peter.

"Henry! Stop it!" shrieked Mum.
"Leave your brother alone."

NAH NAH NE NAH NAH, mouthed Steve behind
Aunt Ruby's back.

"Isn't it *lovely* how nicely the boys are playing together?" said Aunt Ruby.

"Yes, isn't it?" said Mum.

"Not surprising," said Aunt Ruby, beaming. "After all, Steve is such a polite, friendly boy, I've never met anyone who didn't love him."

Snore! Snore! Snore!

Horrid Henry lay on a mattress listening to hideous snoring sounds. He'd stayed awake for hours, just in case they tried anything

HORRIBLE, like pouring water on his head, or stuffing frogs in his bed. Which was what he was going to do to Peter, the moment he got home.

Henry had just spent the most horrible Saturday of his life. He'd **begged** to go to the PAINTBALLING party. He'd **pleaded** to go to the paintballing party. He'd **SCREAMED** about going to the paintballing party. But no. His **MEAN, HORRIBLE** parents wouldn't budge. And it was all Steve and Bill's fault.

They'd **tripped** him going down the stairs.

They'd **kicked** him under the table
at dinner (and then complained that
he was kicking them). And every time
Aunt Ruby's back was turned they
stuck out their tongues and jeered:
"We're going PAINTBALLING,
and you're not."

He had to get to that party. And he
had to be revenged. But how? How?
His two arch-enemies had banded
together and struck the first blow.

Could he **booby-trap** their beds and remove a few slats? Unfortunately, everyone would know he'd done it and he'd be in even more trouble than he was now.

Scare them? Tell them there was a MONSTER under the bed? Hmmm. He knew Steve was as big a scaredy cat as Peter. But he'd already done that once. He didn't think Steve would fall for it again.

Get them into trouble? Turn them against each other? Steal their best toys and hide them? Hmmm. Hmmm.

Horrid Henry thought and thought.
He had to be revenged. He had to.

TWEET TWEET. It was Sunday morning.
The birds were *singing*. The sun was
shining. The—

Yank!

Bossy Bill and STUCK-UP STEVE
pulled off his duvet.

"Nah na ne nah nah, we-ee beat
you," crowed Bill.

"Nah na ne nah nah, we got you into trouble," crowed Steve.

Horrid Henry scowled. Time to put **Operation Revenge** into action.

"Bill thinks you're bossy, Steve," said Henry. "He told me."

"Didn't," said Bossy Bill.

"And Steve thinks you're stuck-up, Bill," added Henry sweetly.

"No I don't," said Steve.

"Then why'd you tell me that?" said Horrid Henry.

Steve stuck his nose in the air.

"Nice try, Henry, you big loser," said

STUCK-UP STEVE. "Just ignore him, Bill."

"Henry, it's not nice to tell lies," said Perfect Peter.

"Shut up, **worm**," snarled Horrid Henry.

RATS.

Time for plan B.

Except he didn't have a plan B.

"I can't wait for Tim's party," said Bossy Bill. "You never know what's going to happen."

"Yeah, remember when he told us he was having a **pirate party** and instead we went to the **Wild West**

Theme Park!" said Steve.

"Or when he said we were having a sleepover, and instead we all went to a **MANIC BUZZARDS** concert."

"And Tim gives the best party bags. Last year everyone got a **Deluxe Demon Dagger Sabre**," said Steve. "Wonder what he'll give this year? Oh, I forgot, Henry won't be coming to the party."

"Too bad you can't come, Henry," sneered Bossy Bill.

"Yeah, too bad," sneered Stuck-Up Steve. "Not."

ARRRRGGGHH. Horrid Henry's blood boiled. He couldn't decide what was worse, listening to them **CROW** about having got him into so much trouble, or hearing them brag about the great **PARTY** they were going to and he wasn't.

"I can't wait to find out what surprises he'll have in store this year," said Bill.

"Yeah," said Steve.

Who cares? thought **Horrid Henry**.

Unless Tim was planning to throw
Bill and Steve into a **shark tank**.
That would be a nice surprise.
Unless of course . . . And then
suddenly Horrid Henry had a *brilliant,*
SPECTACULAR idea. It was so
brilliant, and so **SPECTACULAR**, that
for a moment he wondered whether
he could stop himself from *flinging*
open the window and shouting his

plan out loud. Oh wow. Oh wow. It was risky.

It was dangerous. But if it worked, he would have the best revenge ever in the history of the **WORLD**. No, the history of the **SOLAR SYSTEM**. No, the history of the **UNIVERSE!**

It was an hour before the party. **Horrid Henry** was counting the seconds until he could escape.

Aunt Ruby popped her head round the door, *waving* an envelope.

"Letter for you boys," she said.

Steve **SNATCHED** it and tore it open.

"He must be planning something amazing," said Bill.

Dear Steve and Bill
Party of the year update.
Everyone must come to my house
wearing pyjamas (you'll find
out why later, but don't be
surprised if we all end up in
a film — shhhh). It'll be a real
laugh. Make sure to bring
your favourite soft toys, too,
and wear your fluffiest
slippers. Hollywood, here
we come!

Tim

"I bet we're all going to be acting in a film!" said Steve.

"Yeah!" said Bill.

"Too bad you won't, Henry," said STUCK-UP STEVE.

"You're so LUCKY," said Henry. "I wish I were going."

Mum looked at Dad.

Dad looked at Mum.

Henry held his breath.

"Well, you can't, Henry, and that's final," said Mum.

"IT'S SO UNFAIR!" shrieked Henry.

Henry's parents dropped Steve and Bill off at Tim's party on their way home. Steve was in his *blue bunny pyjamas* and blue bunny fluffy slippers, and clutching a panda.

Bill was in his *yellow duckling pyjamas* and yellow duckling fluffy slippers, and clutching his monkey.

"Shame you can't come, Henry," said Steve, smirking. "But we'll be sure to tell you all about it."

"Do," said Henry, as Mum drove off.

Horrid Henry heard squeals of laughter at Hoity-Toity Tim's front door. Bill and Steve stood frozen. Then they started to wave frantically at the car.

"Are they saying something?" said Mum, glancing in the rear-view mirror.

"Nah, just waving goodbye," said Horrid Henry. He rolled down his window.

"Have fun, guys!"

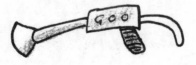

HORRID HENRY

AND THE REVENGE OF THE BOGEY BABYSITTER

"I challenge you to a name-calling competition," shrieked Rude Ralph. "For the title of champion name-caller of the universe."

HA, thought Horrid Henry. No one knew more rude names than Henry. Not even Rude Ralph.

"You're on," said Horrid Henry.

"Woofy."

"Pongy."

"Smelly."

"Whiffy."

"Stinky."

"Reeky."

"Farty."

"Umm . . . Ummm . . ." said Ralph.

"Umm isn't a name," crowed Henry.

"Nah na ne nah nah, I
am champion."

"Shut up, I'm
thinking," said Ralph.

"Poo breath."

"Gloppy goop."

"Smellovision."

"Odiferous."

"Odiferous?

That's not a word,"
said Ralph.

"Is too."

"Is not."

"Wibble pants."

"**Barf breath**."

"Turkey head."

"Turkey head?" said
Rude Ralph.

"Turkey head?
That's not a—"

DING DONG.

Horrid Henry stopped **jumping** up and down on Ralph's bed.

"Who's that?" said Henry.

Ralph shrugged. "We're having a **BABYSITTER** tonight," he said.

Horrid Henry's eyes gleamed.

A **BABYSITTER!** Yeah. What could be better than a sleepover at Ralph's with a **BABYSITTER?** He'd yet to meet one he couldn't tame. After all, he wasn't called the **Bulldozer of Babysitters** for nothing. A sitter meant hours of rampaging **FUN**. Especially as Ralph was bound to have one

of those brilliant BABYSITTERS who let you stay up all night and eat biscuits till you were sick and watch SCARY movies on TV. The kind his mean, HORRIBLE parents never ever got for him.

"Great," said Henry. "Who?" He hoped it would be Leafy Leon. He just sat with his headphones on doing his homework. Or Allergic Alice, who he'd heard was always too busy sneezing to see kids sneaking sweets. Or maybe — oh please please please — Dippy Dora.

Margaret said Dora had spent the whole evening on her phone and hadn't even noticed when Margaret stayed up past midnight and ate all the *ice cream* in the freezer.

"Dunno," said Ralph. "Mum didn't say. Probably Dora."

Yes! thought Horrid Henry.

"And Mum's baked a **chocolate fudge cake**," said Ralph.

"All for us?" said Henry.

"Nah," said Ralph. "Just a slice each."

Ralph looked at Henry.

Henry looked at Ralph.

"You thinking what I'm thinking?" said Henry.

"Oh yeah," said Ralph.

They could **GUZZLE** the whole cake and blame it on the BABYSITTER. What *brilliant* luck, thought **Horrid Henry**. Hmm, boy, he could taste that yummy, **gooey** scrumptious chocolate cake already.

STOMP.

STOMP.

STOMP.

There was the sound of **elephants** trampling.

"What was that?" said Horrid Henry.

BOOM.

BOOM.

BOOM.

The **elephants** were joined by a herd of stampeding **RHINOCEROSES**.

"You don't think . . . " whispered Henry.

"It can't be . . ." whispered Ralph.

The walls **sh**o**ok**.

Henry gasped.

The ground **sh**o**ok**.

Ralph gulped.

"We'd better go and see," said Rude
Ralph.

Henry and Ralph crept down the
stairs and peeked round the door.

AAARRRGHHHHHH!

Stomping towards them was the **BIGGEST**, MEANEST, ugliest **HIDEOUSLY HORRIBLE** teen Henry remembered from his worst nightmares. **Enormous** kid-mashing arms: check. **Enormous** spiky head: check. **Enormous** Henry-hating eyes and child-chewing fangs: check.

It was Rabid Rebecca, the **BOGEY BABYSITTER**, risen from the swamp where she thrashed around with the Loch Ness Monster and the Creature from the Black Lagoon.

"When you said you were having a

BABYSITTER, you never said it could be — Rebecca," hissed Horrid Henry.

"I didn't know," whimpered Rude Ralph.

"We're doomed," moaned Horrid Henry.

"WHERE'S THE FOOD?" bellowed Rabid Rebecca.

Ralph's mum pointed to the kitchen. "The boys can have a SMALL

slice of cake each," she trilled. "Be good," she shouted over her shoulder as she escaped.

Then Rebecca saw Henry.

Henry saw Rebecca.

"**You**," said **Rabid Rebecca**. Her evil eyes narrowed.

"**Me**," said Horrid Henry.

Last time he'd met **Rabid Rebecca** they'd had a fight almost to the death. Henry had hoped never to have a re-match. Then he remembered her weakness . . .

"Don't worry, she's scared of **spiders**,"

whispered Henry. "All we have to do is find some—"

"And don't get any ideas about **spiders**," said Rebecca. "I brought my friend Rachel. Nothing scares her."

Horrid Henry gasped as a terrifying fiend cast a **BLACK SHADOW** over the sitting room. Rancid Rachel was even tougher-looking than **Rabid Rebecca**.

Rancid Rachel *glared* at Henry and Ralph. Her **fangs** gleamed.

"If I were you, I'd get straight upstairs to bed," growled Rachel.

"That way I won't
step on you by
mistake."

"But what about
my chocolate cake?"
squeaked Ralph. "My
mum said—"

"**Our** cake, you
mean," said the **BOGEY
BABYSITTERS**.

"Don't you touch that
cake!" squeaked
Ralph.

"Yeah," said Horrid Henry. "Or else."

Rancid Rachel cracked her knuckles.

"Or else what?" she snarled.

Horrid Henry took a step back.

"Ooh, doesn't that cake look yummy," said Rachel. "Doncha think, Becs?"

"Yeah," said **Rabid Rebecca**. "I can't wait to eat it. Nice of the brat's mum to leave it all for us. Now go to bed before we **EAT** . . . YOU!"

"I'm not moving," said Horrid Henry.

"Yeah," said Rude Ralph. "Make me."

"**GET OUT OF HERE!**" boomed the bogey babysitters, exhaling their dragon breath.

Horrid Henry and Rude Ralph sat in his bedroom. They could hear the **BOGEY BABYSITTERS** cackling and laughing in the kitchen below.

"We've got to stop them stealing all the cake," said Ralph. "It's not fair."

"I know," said Henry.

"But how?" said Ralph. "She told us to stay in bed."

"So what," said **Horrid Henry**. He scowled. There had to be something they could do to stop the *crime of the century.*

"How?" said Ralph. "Call the police?"

Tempting, thought Horrid Henry. But somehow he didn't think the police would be too keen to race over and arrest two **HORRIBLE** babysitters for scoffing a cake.

"We could tell Rebecca it's poisoned," said Ralph.

"What, your mum made you a poisoned cake?" said Henry. "Don't think they'd believe you."

Rude Ralph hung his head.

"It's hopeless," said Ralph. "Now we won't get any."

No cake? No **YUMMY** chocolate cake dripping with fudgy frosting and studded with sweets?

Horrid Henry wasn't the **SQUISHER OF SITTERS** for nothing. Wasn't there some film he'd seen, or story he'd heard, where . . . where . . .

"Get some keys and some string," said Henry. "And one of your dad's suits on a hanger. Hurry."

"Why?" said Ralph.

"Do you want that cake or don't you?" said Henry. "Now do exactly what I say."

"AAAAARRGGGHHHH!"

The blood-curdling scream echoed through the house.

AAAAAARRRGGGGHHHHHHH!

AAAAAARRRGGGGHHHHHHH!

AAAAAARRRGGGGHHHHHHH!

Trudge.

      Trudge.

            Trudge.

Rabid Rebecca flung open Ralph's bedroom door. She *glared* at them screaming and trembling in the corner and flashed her **child-chewing** fangs.

"Stop screaming, you little creeps," snarled **Rabid Rebecca**. "Or I'll give you something to scream about."

"We saw . . . we saw . . ." gasped Ralph.

"A **headless ghost**," gasped Henry. "Outside the window."

Rabid Rebecca snorted.

"Yeah, right," she said. "Now shut up and go to sleep."

She left, slamming the door behind her.

"Go!" said Horrid Henry.

Horrid Henry ran into the kitchen, panting and gasping.

There were the **BOGEY BABYSITTERS**, huddled over the cake. One slice was already gone.

Rabid Rebecca looked up, cake knife in hand.

"I smell a child," she hissed.

"What are you doing down here?" roared Rancid Rachel. "Go away before we—"

"I'm **SCARED**," said Horrid Henry. "I heard a noise."

"You're just trying to make an

excuse to get out of bed, you little **worm**," said Rebecca.

"You'd better get out of here before I count to three," bellowed Rachel. **"OR ELSE."**

"There's something outside," said Henry.

"ONE TWO THR—"

Clink.

Clink.

Clink.

The clinking noise was coming from outside the kitchen window.

"There," whimpered Horrid Henry. He backed away.

"What was that?" said Rebecca, the cake halfway to her drooling jaws.

"Nothing," said Rachel, shoving a huge bit in her mouth.

Clink.

    Clink.

        Clink.

Rachel stopped chewing.

"That," hissed **Rabid Rebecca**. "That clinking noise."

"I told you there's something outside," whispered Horrid Henry.

BANG.

BANG.

BANG.

Rancid Rachel stood up.

"Ahh, it's just the wind," she said.

BANG.

BANG.

BANG.

"I'll show you," said Rachel. "I'm not scared."

She marched over to the window and drew back the curtain.

There in the dark was a headless suit, flapping and rapping at the window.

"**AAARRRGGGHHH!**" screeched Rebecca. She spat out her mouthful.

"**AAARRRGGGHHH!**" screeched Rachel. She spat out her mouthful.

"It's a **GHOST!** Hide!" they howled, racing from the kitchen and clambering up the stairs.

"Go outside and see what it is," screamed Horrid Henry.

"No way," shrieked Rebecca.

They barricaded themselves into the bathroom and locked the door.

Horrid Henry snatched the cake off the cake stand and *raced* back to Ralph's room.

Ralph was standing at the open window, dangling a hanger from a string with his dad's suit on it.

Henry beamed at Ralph as he hauled in the suit and untied the keys he'd used to clink on the ground.

Ralph *beamed* at Henry.

"Good job, partner," said Henry, helping himself to a **gigantic** piece of chocolate cake. Hmmm, boy, it was delicious.

"Good job, partner," said Ralph, digging into an even **BIGGER** one.

"Won't your mum be furious with Rebecca when she comes home and finds all the cake gone?" mumbled Henry, taking another enormous slice.

"Boy will she ever," said Ralph. "I bet Rebecca never babysits here again."

HORRID HENRY'S
BAD BOOK

"Henry. Get down here."

"Henry. We're waiting for you."

"I'm READING!" bellowed Horrid Henry.

How could he go out with his mean, HORRIBLE parents before he found out what Evil Evie would do next?

Evil Evie came up with the best tricks. The time she pretended to be allergic to vegetables! Or put slugs in her sister's slippers for April Fool's Day! Or swapped her parents. Or

saved the planet by
refusing to take baths.
Or won the **LOTTERY**
and spent every penny on
toys and chocolate. Or rode in the car
with a pot of lasagne on her lap and
accidentally took the lid off . . .

WOW.

Why couldn't he have a *brilliant* sister
like Evie instead of a waste of space
wormy ToAD brother like Peter?

"Not those awful books again," said Dad.
"Can't you find anything better to

read?" said Mum.

"These are the *best books ever*," said Horrid Henry.

"Too ᵐᵉᴬᴺ," said Mum.

"Too aggressive," said Dad.

Horrid Henry sighed.

First, his parents complained that he only read comics. Then, after he'd discovered the *best books ever* in the history of the universe and couldn't stop reading them over and over and over again, and even bought them with his own **PRECIOUS** pocket money, his parents complained that they hated the Evil Evie series.

"Such a bad example," said Mum.

"They put ideas into his head," said Dad.

"Why can't you read books about good children who always obey their parents?" they moaned.

Horrid Henry rolled his eyes. Wasn't reading meant to be about **FUN** and **adventure** and *escape?* He got enough real life in real life.

Horrid Henry loved Evil Evie.

Rude Ralph loved Evil Evie.

MOODY MARGARET loved Evil Evie.

In fact, **EVERYONE** at school loved Evil Evie.

Even **MISS BATTLE-AXE** loved the Evil Evie books and read her adventures out loud every day during story time. Evil Evie and the Roaring Rogues. Evil

Evie and the Tyrant Teacher. Evil Evie and the Mad Scientist. Evil Evie, Pirate Queen.

They were definitely the funniest books ever. **Horrid Henry** could win any **Evil Evie** competition. He knew everything about her.

Her favourite vegetable: **ketchup**.

Her catch-phrase: **BUZZ OFF, ~~BANANA-HEAD~~**.

Her favourite word: *swashbuckling*.

 Her favourite colour: purple (just like his).

Her favourite **TV**

programme: *Robot Riot.*

Her **evilest** enemies: Rotten Robert, the **MONSTER** next door, and Snobby Bobby, her stuck-up cousin.

Her secret job: Spy Assassin.

Her **FOUL** sister: Wilting Willa, an infant fiend in training.

Her pet rat: Doris.

Her hometown: Rudeville.

Her ~~MEAN, HORRIBLE~~ parents. Hmmm, they didn't appear to have names. Probably because they were so old they'd forgotten them, thought Horrid Henry.

Evil Evie was **Horrid Henry's** Mastermind subject.

Best of all, every time Henry got into trouble, he blamed Evil Evie.

"Evie did that," he squealed when Mum told him off for poking Peter.

"Evie did that," he shrieked when Dad told him off for calling Peter names.

"Evie did that," lied Henry when Mum and Dad told him off for calling the police when **MISS BATTLE-AXE** refused to give him sweets.

After all, his parents hadn't read

the Evil Evie
books, had
they? How
would they
know?

Tee hee.

"Mum!" squealed Peter. "Henry
called me wimpadoodle and *wibble
wobble pants*."

"Stop being **HORRID**, Henry,"
said Mum.

"Henry was never **HORRID**
until he started reading those
horrible books," said Dad.

"Those books are a bad influence," said Mum. "He always played *nicely* with Peter before."

"Really?" said Grandma. "I don't remember that."

From next door came the sound of slapping.

"**I HATE YOU**, Susan," screamed Margaret.

"**I hate you more**," screamed Susan.

Moody Margaret's mum leaned over

the garden wall.

"You know how my little Maggie Moo Moo has always been the sweetest, kindest, QUIETEST child ever," said her mother. "A jewel. Perfect in every way. Well, ever since she discovered Evil Evie, she's become . . . a total TERROR."

"Henry too," said Mum. "I'm sure he'd play beautifully with his brother if those books hadn't put ideas into his head."

"I'm sick and tired of these TERRIBLE books," said Margaret's mother. "Margaret's become so **MOODY** since she started reading them."

Horrid Henry looked up from his book, **Evil Evie Stings the Scorpion.**

"Margaret's been a moody old grouch since she was a tadpole," said Henry.

"Don't be **HORRID**, Henry," said Mum.

"I never read **Evil Evie**," said Peter. "I'd much rather read about good children."

"Quite right, Peter," said Mum.

Horrid Henry pounced.

He was a giant mosquito *dive-bombing* for his supper.

"Aiieeeeee!" squealed Peter. "Henry pinched me."

"Evil Evie did that to her sister," said Horrid Henry. "I was just copying her."

Tee hee. Evil Evie was the best get-out-of-jail-free card ever.

Horrid Henry walked into his bedroom after a long day at school.

Phew.

Finally, a chance to relax on his bed with a favourite **Evil Evie**, maybe **Evil Evie** and the Dastardly Demon—

Huh?

His special Evil Evie bookcase was empty.

"Where are my **Evil Evie** books?" shrieked Henry. "Someone's stolen them."

"Banned," said Mum, coming into the room.

"Banned," said Dad. "We're sick and tired of your **HORRID** copy cat behaviour."

Oops.

Horrid Henry hadn't thought of that. He thought he'd been brilliant blaming everything on Evie. And now his brilliance had backfired.

"But I want to read," wailed Horrid Henry.

"And that's why we've got a present for you, Henry," said Mum. "The

fabulous *Gallant Gary* series. Much
better than Evil Evie. Margaret's mum
recommended them."

She handed Henry a book with a
sparkling silver cover. There was a
picture of a boy holding a tea towel,
with a halo framing his brown curls.

"Gallant . . .
Gary?" said
Horrid Henry.
He read the story
titles.

BLECCCCCHHH.

Horrid Henry opened the book as if it were **radioactive** and flicked through the **grisly** pages.

There was *Gallant Gary* helping an old lady across the street.

There was *Gallant Gary* telling his mum to rest her feet while he cleared the table and did loads of chores.

There was *Gallant Gary* playing catch with his adorable younger brother Little Larry.

BLECCCCCHHH.

Horrid Henry slammed the book shut.

UGGGH.

Didn't he have enough *goody goodies* in his life with Peter?

"These stories are **BORING**," said
Henry. "I want my Evil Evie books
back."

"Maybe you'll learn something," said
Mum.

"Maybe you'll stop being so
HORRID," said Dad.

"Why don't you copy *Gary?*"
said Mum. "That would be
wonderful."

"**NO!**" screamed Henry.

At lunchtime **Horrid Henry** went to his school library. Why hadn't he thought of this before? TRALALA, he'd check out some **Evil Evie** books and cover them with *Gallant Gary* covers. TRALALA, a trick worthy of Evie herself . . .

What?

The **Evil Evie** shelf was empty.

"All the **Evil Evie** books are checked out, I'm afraid," said the librarian, Beaming Bea. "I have lots of *Gallant Gary* if you want to try something new."

"**NOOOOOOO**," said Horrid Henry. "I want to read **Evil Evie!!**"

"You and everyone else," said the librarian.

He had to get his books back. He had to. He couldn't get to sleep without an Evil Evie book. He couldn't relax after school without an Evil Evie book.

Why had he ever blamed Evie for being **HORRID?** What would Evie do in this dreadful situation?

And then suddenly **Horrid Henry** had a brilliant, SPECTACULAR

idea. It was
so *brilliant*, and so
SPECTACULAR,
that Henry started
dancing around the
library, whooping and
cheering.

"Shhh," said Beaming Bea, frowning.

What was it Mum had said? Why
didn't he copy Gary?

Copy *Gallant Gary*, thought Henry.
Copy *Gallant Gary*. **BOY** could he copy
Gallant Gary.

On their way to the park **Horrid Henry** grabbed Grandma and tugged on her arm.

"I'm helping you cross the road," he shouted.

"But I don't want to cross the road," said Grandma.

"Too bad," said Henry, *yanking* her. "You're an old lady and you're crossing."

"HELP!" squealed Grandma.

"Henry, stop that at once," shouted Mum.

Henry stopped. "But I'm only copying *Gary*, like you said. He's always helping old ladies cross the road."

Mum opened her mouth and then closed it.

SQUELCH SQUERCH.

"Mum!" squealed Peter.

Mum ran into the sitting room.
Great globs of SOAPY SUDS
bubbled from the carpet up to
Peter's knees.

"What's going on?" said Mum.
"Henry! What have
you done?" she
said, looking
at the
bubbling
carpet.

"I was just copying *Gary*," said
Henry, squirting more shampoo. "I
know you wanted to shampoo
the carpet and I was trying to
help you with your chores, just
like *Gary*."

"Stop," said Mum, as her feet sank
in the suds. "Uhhm, thank you
Henry, that's enough."

That night, after supper, Horrid
Henry leapt to his feet.

"I'll clear," said Horrid Henry,
gathering all the dirty plates and
heading towards the kitchen.

CRASH SMASH

Broken plates cascaded round the floor.

"Henry!" shouted Dad.

"I'm copying *Gary*, just like you said," said Henry. "He always clears the table."

"Oh," said Mum.

"Oh," said Dad.

"C'mon, Peter, let's play catch in the garden," said Horrid Henry.

Perfect Peter stared. Henry never offered to play with him.

Mum smiled. "Yes, go on, Peter," she said.

"Just like *Gallant Gary* and Little Larry," said Henry, hurling the ball.

The ball torpedoed through the kitchen window.

CRASH.

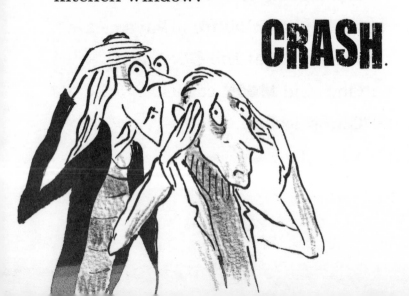

Glass splinters flew
everywhere as the
window shattered.

"HENRY!"
screamed Mum
and Dad.

"I'm so sorry," said Horrid Henry.
"I was just copying *Gary*. He and Little
Larry are always playing catch."

Mum looked at Dad.

Dad looked at Mum.

They stared at the **BROKEN**
window, the **soapy** carpet and the
smashed dishes.

"Don't worry," said Horrid Henry. "I'll keep copying *Gary*, just like you said."

"Oh," said Mum.

"Oh," said Dad.

Horrid Henry came home from school the next day and walked slowly up to his bedroom. No . No chance to relax with an **Evil Evie** book—

Henry stared. His special bookshelf was full. Packed to the brim with

Evil Evie books.

Evil Evie was back. *Gary* was gone.

YIPPEE!!!!!!

Horrid Henry picked up
his favourite book and lay
back on his bed.

He turned to the first
page and began to read.

Evie was evil.

Everyone said so, even
her mother.

HORRID HENRY

PRANK WARS

Turn the
page for some
SUPER SILLY
bonus games and
activities!

April Fool's WordSearch

HENRY LOVES APRIL FOOL'S DAY! CAN YOU FIND THE
EIGHT HIDDEN WORDS IN THIS WORDSEARCH?

**Prankster - Fool - Hijinks - Joke -
Gullible - Spoof - Hoax - Trick**

G	G	Q	X	S	R	Y	Z	P	A	L	V	P	L	H
T	M	F	M	Y	N	T	D	R	G	B	I	H	T	U
D	S	H	S	B	T	I	Z	A	B	V	W	T	H	X
H	B	K	X	H	I	J	I	N	K	S	T	J	I	L
Y	E	I	I	T	Y	O	E	K	K	Y	V	Y	E	K
N	S	A	B	O	T	K	G	S	N	R	M	D	F	Z
G	M	S	W	B	T	E	P	T	R	N	O	C	Y	E
I	U	W	R	J	S	H	L	E	P	E	U	M	Q	O
S	Y	L	E	T	E	R	T	R	I	C	K	B	N	P
A	J	M	L	S	K	U	L	O	B	A	W	G	E	S
V	N	U	H	I	W	M	C	O	S	F	M	S	W	A
N	W	E	C	O	B	G	O	R	F	T	F	P	N	T
I	F	X	F	O	O	L	Q	D	B	B	H	O	A	X
N	C	X	B	F	D	Y	E	R	A	L	G	O	U	B
H	D	N	I	P	Y	D	R	I	O	G	Y	F	U	P

PRANK KING

HENRY IS THE PRANK KING! WHY NOT TRY SOME OF HENRY'S FAVOURITE PRANKS ON YOUR FRIENDS AND FAMILY?

SUPER SWEET

Offer them a glass of water and when they're not looking, put a spoonful of sugar in it. It will be a sweet surprise!

BALLOON DROP

Blow up a couple of balloons and balance them on top of a door that is open ajar. Call your victim into the room. When they open the door, the balloons will drop on them, giving them a scare.

PRANKS SHOULD BE FUN AND NOT HURT OR UPSET ANYONE!

FAKE FART
Place a whoopie cushion under a sofa cushion. When your victim sits down it will let out a loud fart sound!

PRRRRR

TIME TWIST
Set their alarm clock an hour early so they wake up thinking they're late and run around getting ready. Make sure you tell them the clock's wrong when you've finished laughing!

CRISP SUPRISE
Fill an empty bag of crisps with jelly, then offer them a crisp. They'll put their hand in and have a slimey surprise!

TONGUE TWISTERS

TRY TO BEAT YOUR FRIENDS AT THESE SUPER TRICKY TONGUE TWISTERS.

1. The big bug bit the little beetle
2. Kids and kittens knit in the kitchen
3. Laughing Lucie lost loads of loot
4. Red lorry yellow lorry
5. She sells seashells by the seashore
6. Can clams cram cans of candy?

ODD MONSTER OUT

DO YOU KNOW YOUR ZOMBIE VAMPIRE FROM YOUR FANGMANGLER? WHICH MONSTER DOESN'T HAVE A PAIR IN THE PICTURES?

PRACTICAL JOKES

TRY OUT THESE SIDE-SPLITTING JOKES ON YOUR
FRIENDS AND FAMILY!

1. Which monster plays the best pranks?

   Prankenstein

2. What did zero say to eight?

   Nice belt!

3. Who's in charge of the pencil case?

   The ruler!

4. Do you know about April 1st?

   Yes, I'm fooly aware of it!

5. What is green and not heavy?

Light green!

6. What do you call a fake lasagne?

An impasta!

7. Who did the zombie take to the dance?

His ghoul-friend

8. What is a stepladder's favourite day?

April Stool's Day!

Who Am I?

DO YOU KNOW YOUR ANXIOUS ANDREWS FROM YOUR BRAINY BRIANS? CAN YOU WORK OUT WHO EACH OF THESE CHARACTERS ARE?

1. My brother is very mean and always calls me a worm. I'm the leader of the Best Boys Club.

2. I'm the fastest boy at school and love sports!

3. I dunno.

4. I am a teacher and Henry's class is the worst I have ever taught – and Henry is by far the worst child!

5. Henry and Peter are my cousins. They're very poor and don't get nearly as many presents as I do.

6. La la la – I love singing!

7. I'm the best girl in the world – I'm the smartest, the fastest and the most talented. The Secret Club is way better than the Purple Hand Gang!

8. I love Henwy. I want to mawwy him.

9. Meow.

10. I love being a teacher – my class are so … lovely!

Crossword Hijinks

HENRY AND RALPH ARE UP TO MISCHIEF. CAN YOU WORK OUT WHAT PRANKS THEY'RE GOING TO PLAY?

ACROSS

2. AN INSECT WITH EIGHT LEGS
5. HENRY'S USUAL VICTIM
6. HENRY PRETENDED THERE WAS ONE OF THESE IN HIS GARDEN
7. SOMETHING GREEN THAT COMES FROM YOUR NOSE
9. HENRY'S FAVOURITE SLIMY TOY

DOWN

1. WET PAPER SCRUNCHED IN A BALL
3. USE THIS TO SHOOT SPITBALLS
4. YOU FILL UP BALLOONS TO MAKE THESE
5. HENRY'S ALWAYS PLANNING ONE OF THESE
8. AN INGREDIENT FOR MAKING BREAD

MAKE YOUR OWN MONSTER!

FOLLOW THESE EASY SIX STEPS TO CREATE YOUR OWN MONSTEROUS DISGUISE!

You will need:
Two cushions
A big T-shirt
A belt
A mop head

1. Hold one cushion on your front and one on your back.

2. Ask for some help buckling the belt around your middle to keep the cushions secure.

3. Now put on a big T-shirt to cover up the cushions.

4. Wear the dry mop head on your head like a hat.

5. Now find a good spot to jump out at someone (try behind the sofa!).

6. Jump out and do your scariest roar. See how high your friends jump!

BONUS STEP:
If you have fake teeth or face paint you can use these to make yourself even scarier!

SILLY SUDOKU

HENRY'S CHANGED ALL THE NUMBERS IN PETER'S SUDOKU TO SILLY PICTURES. HELP PETER COMPLETE THE SUDOKU PUZZLES.

SPOT THE DIFFERENCE

HAVE YOU EVER SEEN A ZOMBIE, A VAMPIRE AND A WEREWOLF ARM WRESTLE? SPOT THE FIVE DIFFERENCES BETWEEN THE TWO PICTURES.

ANSWERS

April Fool's Wordsearch

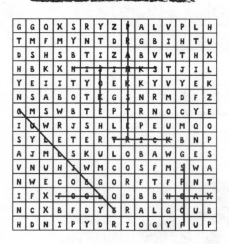

G	G	Q	X	S	R	Y	Z	A	A	L	V	P	L	H
T	M	F	M	Y	N	T	D	R	G	B	I	H	T	U
D	S	H	S	B	T	I	Z	A	B	V	W	T	H	X
H	B	K	X	H	I	J	I	N	K	S	T	J	I	L
Y	E	I	I	T	Y	O	E	K	K	Y	V	Y	E	K
N	S	A	B	O	T	E	G	S	N	R	M	D	F	Z
O	M	S	W	B	T	E	P	T	R	N	O	C	Y	E
I	U	W	R	J	S	H	L	E	P	E	U	M	Q	O
S	Y	L	E	T	E	R	T	R	I	C	K	B	N	P
A	J	M	L	S	K	U	L	O	B	A	W	G	E	S
V	N	U	H	I	W	M	C	O	S	F	M	S	W	A
N	W	E	C	O	B	G	O	R	F	T	F	P	N	T
I	F	X	F	O	O	L	Q	D	B	B	H	C	A	X
N	C	X	B	F	D	Y	B	R	A	L	G	Q	U	B
H	D	N	I	P	Y	D	R	I	O	G	Y	P	U	P

Odd Monster Out

Who Am I?

1. Perfect Peter
2. Aerobic Al
3. Beefy Bert
4. Miss Battle-Axe
5. Stuck-Up Steve
6. Singing Soraya
7. Moody Margaret
8. Lisping Lily
9. Fluffy
10. Miss Lovely

Crossword Hijinx

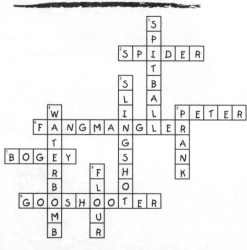

Silly Sudoku

Spot the Difference

COLLECT ALL THE
HORRID HENRY STORYBOOKS!